GEETA AND THE VILLAGE SCHOOL

W9-DFD-330

GEETA AND

VILLAGE

b

with illustrations

by Ronni Solbert

THE
SCHOOL

arvathi Thampi

UBLEDAY & COMPANY, INC., GARDEN CITY, NEW YORK

Copyright © 1960 by Parvathi Thampi
Illustrations Copyright © 1960 by Ronni Solbert
Library of Congress Catalog Card Number 60-7140
All Rights Reserved.
Lithographed in the United States of America.
First Edition.

GEETA AND THE VILLAGE SCHOOL

CO. SCHOOLS

C498550

Chapter opening decorations were copied from wall paintings and floor designs made in clay, which are found almost everywhere in the villages of India—even in the poorest huts. Made by members of the household, usually a mother or daughter, many are the householder's own designs or variations on ones handed down from one generation to another.

GEETA was playing with her friends in the main square of the little village in India where she lived. Suddenly she stopped running and stood still and looked up at the sky. Her best friend, Kamala, touched her on the shoulder and said, "Tag, Geeta, you're It," but Geeta didn't even hear her.

Geeta was looking at a big dark cloud in the sky. The cloud was moving toward the sun and casting a shadow on the hot square, and Geeta was afraid of the cloud.

"Tag, Geeta," Kamala said again, and the others said, "What's the matter, Geeta?" and they said, "Come on, Geeta, you're It."

Geeta wanted to tell them she couldn't play any longer. She wanted to tell them she was afraid of the big dark cloud. But she was too shy and she was sure they would all laugh at her.

"Try and catch me, Geeta," Kamala said and she started to run across the square.

Then the big dark cloud sailed right across the sun and Gopu, the oldest and biggest of them all,

shouted, "Look! Look! It's going to rain. Hurrah! Hurrah! Hurrah!"

The others looked up and the big cloud split open like a monster's mouth and sent out a tongue of forked blue lightning, and Gopu held out his hand and shouted, "Come, lightning, come into my hand!"

All Geeta's friends jumped up and down and clapped their hands. They were glad that the rain was coming to cool the hot, dry air and make the crops grow so that they would have food. But Geeta was not glad because she was afraid of the big cloud and the lightning.

She was so afraid she could not move at all until thunder broke out of the cloud in a terrible burst of sound. Then Geeta ran as fast as she could toward her own house beyond the square. The others called after her, "Come back, Geeta, come back and watch for the rain to come. We'll play in the rain, Geeta, and be cool," but Geeta did not hear them because she was too frightened to hear anything but the terrible thunder.

She kept on running until she came to her own house and to her mother, who was standing on the

porch. Geeta hid her face against her mother so she would not see the lightning and she pulled her mother's dress around her ears. But she could not shut out the terrible sound of the thunder.

Then Geeta's mother took her inside the house and spoke softly to her. "Do not be afraid, my timid fawn," she said. But Geeta was still so frightened she was shaking all over.

Her mother said, "Listen to me, Geeta. You know your name means 'a song' and you know how everything sings in our village. The cocks sing at sunrise and the birds sing in the morning and in the evening. The flute sings when your big brother Balan plays it and the rain sings when it comes with water to the earth and makes our crops grow. The thunder is only the song of clouds that bring rain."

Geeta was still and she thought of what her mother said. She loved the quiet songs of her village where every day the fathers worked in the fields and the mothers worked in the homes and the boys helped the fathers and the girls helped the mothers. But she was not sure the thunder was a song. She thought it was only a great loud noise that made her afraid.

Another clap filled the room and the house and the village. It was the loudest of all and Geeta was so frightened she began to cry.

"Hush," her mother said. "Hush, Geeta, and listen. Listen to the rain pouring over the thirsty earth. There will be no more thunder today."

And Geeta listened and heard the song of the rain and she stopped crying.

"Come, Geeta," her mother said, "come and help me."

Geeta smiled and forgot to be afraid. Though she was only six and could not cook and clean and carry things, she loved to help her mother sift the grain from the chaff and bathe the buffalo and grind the betel nut for grandfather to chew because he was so old he had lost all his teeth and everything had to be mashed fine for him, as it was for babies.

"The very old are like the very young," Geeta's mother said, as they ground the betel nut together, and Geeta laughed and nodded her head because she had forgotten the thunder and because she always agreed with whatever her mother said.

ONE DAY, when the rains had stopped, Geeta and her mother and her father and her little baby brother and her big brother Balan put on their newest clothes because there was going to be a festival. They went to the temple to offer incense and flowers to the good God who sent them rain and food. Geeta felt proud and solemn as she put her flowers with the rest.

After they had made their offerings and said their thanks, everybody in the village went out into the main square and there was plenty to eat and there were music and firecrackers and dancing.

16

Geeta liked to eat the food and listen to the music. She liked the pleasant shivery feeling that went along the middle of her back when the firecrackers went CRACK and she liked to watch the dancing.

17

But the thing she liked best about the festival was the night when all the people lit hundreds of oil lamps in coconut shells till the whole village shone like a starlit sky. One day, she thought, she would be old enough to light her own lamp on festival night.

Geeta loved the festivals but she loved the other times in her village when everything was peaceful and quiet. Usually every day was like every other day except sometimes when a new baby was born or a young woman got married. Then there was much excitement. Geeta thought getting mar-

ried must be the most exciting thing in the world and she always stayed as close to the bride as possible so she could feel her soft new clothes and watch her shining jewels and her shining eyes.

Once a month Geeta stood outside the door of her house and waved good-by to her father when he went to the big city of Madras to sell and buy things and bring back news of the great world outside. Geeta and Balan never got tired of hearing about this world and she could hardly wait through the two long days her father was away. As soon as he came home she grabbed the newspapers wrapped around the things he had brought back from the city and ran with them to Balan. Geeta and Balan could not read the strange writing in the papers but they looked at the pictures, and Geeta wondered and wondered about the great world outside.

One day Geeta's father brought home a paper with a picture of a Thing with a body and wings like a bird, and yet Geeta knew it was not a bird. She asked Balan what the Thing was but Balan shook his head because he did not know. She asked her mother but her mother did not know either. She waited until her father came back from telling

19

the other fathers what he had seen in the town and she said, "Father, what is this Thing?" Her father looked long at the picture, then he said slowly, "They say in the town it is the Silver Bird. It has no life but it moves and flies very fast. It even carries people through the sky."

Geeta's eyes got very big and very round and very bright when she heard this. She did not forget the words but she wondered and wondered about their meaning. What a wonderful place the world

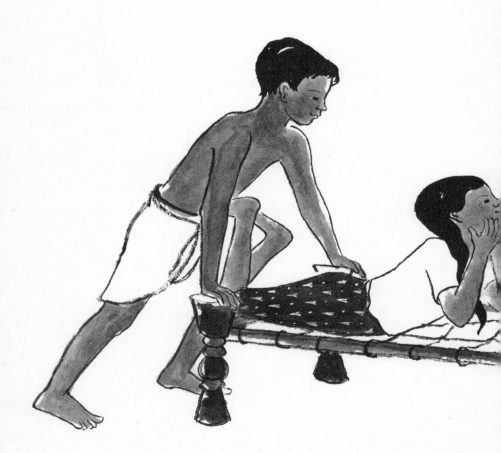

outside must be, she thought, if it could have such things as Silver Birds that did not live but could fly fast in the sky and carry people. She wished she could know more about the great world.

Then—one morning when everything was quiet and peaceful as usual—the great world outside came into the village. Geeta had helped her mother separate the wheat from the chaff and wash the buffalo and grind the betel nut for grandfather and she thought she would go and play with her best friend

Kamala. She came out of the door of her house into the bright day and she saw a big motorcar come roaring into their village. Quickly Geeta hid beside the doorpost and watched. She watched while men with loud voices stepped out of the motorcar. She watched while they talked to her father and to the other fathers. And she watched while they measured the bare patch of land where she and her friends played tag. Then they went away and Geeta wondered what those men with the loud voices were doing in the village. But she didn't ask Balan or her mother or her father because she was afraid they would laugh at her.

But, a few days later, when the men came again with trucks and white bricks and spades and shovels and steam engines and ladders she didn't have to ask and she didn't have to wonder any more because her father told her and Balan and her mother and her little baby brother (who didn't pay much attention because he was really too young to understand). Her father said the men were going to use the spades and shovels and trucks and white bricks and ladders and steam engines to make a great new building right in the middle of their village.

GEETA thought the great new building right in the middle of their village was almost as exciting as a bride. When nobody was looking she ran her fingers over the rough bricks and laid her cheek along the cool panes of glass that would be its windows. Every night she went to sleep thinking about it and every morning she and her friends gathered in the main square to watch the men working on it. Day by day the building grew till it was big and shiny and white. Geeta had never before seen a house like it. It was so different from their own huts with the thatched roofs and the mud floors that she could hardly believe her own eyes.

Geeta and her friends clambered onto the trucks and sometimes they got messy with the sticky gray paste Balan called "cement," and Geeta was sure she had never before in her life had so much fun. There was a lot of noise and dust and there were many different kinds of men. One of them

wore dark glasses and a hat and had a pencil stuck behind his ear. Geeta thought he looked fierce. She was afraid of him and she was glad he did not come very often to the village.

Another of the men wore a bright yellow turban, which made Geeta feel glad because it was so pretty. Another made her laugh, secretly to herself, because his head was so bald and shiny it looked like an egg. And a fourth made them all laugh, right out loud. He had a long drooping mustache that seemed to get in the way of his food when he ate his lunch.

Geeta had never seen such busy men. They hammered and sawed and pounded all morning long. She wondered if they ever got tired. But at lunch time they left their work and they left the building to dream in the sun all by itself and they sat in the shade of the mango grove, opened their packets of rice cakes and lentils wrapped in leaves, and ate and talked to the children. Geeta liked this time best of all the day.

Sometimes one of the men threw a cake to them and then Balan and Kamala and the rest dashed and snatched and pulled. But Geeta only watched them. "I wish I were as big and brave as Balan," she thought. "Then, maybe, I could get the cake." She was hungry, she thought to herself. Everybody she knew was always a little hungry. She started one day to join in the tussle for the cake and then she sighed and stood on one side because she was only six and she knew she was afraid of getting hurt.

"How do you like your new building?" the man with the bright turban asked them one day and Geeta, who was squatting on her heels, nearly fell over into the dust of the main square in surprise.

"Ours?" they said all together.

"Yes, yours," said the man with the drooping mustache. "This building will be your first school."

School. Geeta whispered it to herself. She had never heard that word and it sounded very strange. She wondered if this school was something that belonged to the great world outside like the Silver Bird. She wanted to ask the man with the drooping mustache but she was too shy. She looked at her best friend Kamala and Kamala looked at the others. Then everyone looked at Gopu, the biggest of them all, because Gopu (though he never had a clean face or an untorn shirt) was strong and brave and their leader.

"What is a school?" Gopu asked boldly.

The men laughed loudly. "Ha-ha. Don't you know what a school is? Ha-ha."

But Gopu, because he was strong and brave asked again, "What is a school?"

Now the men did not laugh. They began to hem and haw and Geeta thought to herself, "I bet they don't know either."

Then the one with the yellow turban cleared his throat HARRUMPH and said, "Mind you, we've never been to a school ourselves, but I have heard it is a place where you have to be clean *all the time*."

Geeta did not like this idea. She looked at her clothes and they were dusty and spotted with the gray paste called "cement." She looked at her hands and her feet and they were dusty from the dust in the main square. But the dust felt good and she was comfortable. It was nice to be clean sometimes, she thought, but who would want to be clean all the time?

The man with the hanging mustache said, "And I have heard that a school is like a jail but you can go home at night."

Geeta liked that even less and she felt a little shiver go along her back. She had never been in a jail but she had heard the fathers talk. She thought she did not want to be locked up all the day away

from the sun and the clean air and the buffalo and the wheat and Grandfather's betel nut even if she could go home at night. She began to feel very uncomfortable.

The man who was quite bald said, "They say a school is a place where you have to do exactly as you are told or the teacher will—WHACK!" He shouted the last word and slapped his hand on his bare leg.

Geeta turned and ran home as fast as she could and her heart was as heavy as the buffalo. She remembered how she had watched this white shiny building grow, brick by brick and wall by wall and window by window. She had dreamed of it at night and she thought it was a part of the great world outside and she had thought it was beautiful as she had imagined the great world outside was beautiful. And now she found out it wasn't that way at all. A school was a terrible place where she would be locked up all day (though she could go home at night), where she had to be clean *all the time* and do exactly as she was told or a strange something called Teacher would—WHACK!

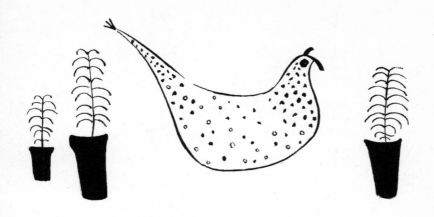

FOR A LONG TIME that night Geeta could not sleep. She knew it was not the mosquitos or her grandfather's snoring that kept her awake because these things she was used to. It was something else, something new and frightening.

School-Teacher-School-Teacher. The words went round and round in her mind till she was all upset and confused. She wanted to talk to Balan but he was fast asleep and even though she pinched his toes he did not wake up. Her baby brother was awake, sucking his thumb, but he would not understand anything, being much too small. She wanted to go to her mother but she could hear her mother and her father talking in the next room and of course you never disturbed fathers and mothers when they were talking to each other. She pressed her ears to the wall to hear what they were saying so she would not feel so alone and afraid.

"The new school will be ready next week," her father's voice said. "I am glad for Balan's sake."

Then her mother's voice said, "And for Geeta's sake too. The school is for both boys and girls."

Geeta held her breath and listened very carefully as her mother said these words. She could not believe her own ears. Surely her *mother* didn't want her to go to that terrible place!

"That is what they say but I am her father and no daughter of mine is going to a school."

Geeta let her breath out fast. She could have hugged her father for saying that. But her mother was speaking again.

"Why not?" her mother said. "We don't even have to pay for it."

Geeta felt a shiver run up and down her back and she set her small white teeth into her lower lip to keep from shouting "NO! NO! NO!"

Then, very clearly, her father said, "Because my daughter is not going to get fancy ideas in her head going to school. As long as she can cook and clean

house and look after the buffalo that's enough for a girl. Did you or your mother ever go to school? No! And you are as good a wife and mother as any woman."

Geeta did not understand all the words but she understood that her father was not going to make her go to the school and she was happy and contented.

But only for a minute. Her mother cleared her throat which she always did when she had something very special to say and her mother said, "I would like Geeta, even though she is a girl, to go to a school and learn things. It is good for her and good for the country. They say the Minister himself is coming to open the school."

There was a long silence and Geeta could feel her heart go thud-thud-thud-thud. What would her father say? Would he make her go to the school because her mother wanted her to?

Then, at last, her father spoke. "For your sake, then, I will ask Geeta if she wants to go to this school. If she says 'Yes,' let her go, but if she says 'No,' let her stay home. As you say, times have changed, so let the girl make up her own mind."

Then Geeta smiled happily to herself in the

dark. She knew she would never say "Yes" and she knew her father would not make her go to the school. And, thinking this, she fell fast asleep.

The next day Geeta's father asked her if she would like to go to the new school and Geeta said "No" in a clear, firm voice. Her mother begged and pleaded with her but Geeta set her chin stubbornly and still said "No," though she felt sad that, for the first time in her life, she did not agree with what her mother said. Geeta saw the hurt and disappointment in her mother's eyes and because she loved her mother so much she could not bear to see her hurt and she ran out of the house.

CO. SCHOOLS
C498550

She went to the house of her best friend Kamala. Kamala was the potter's daughter and she was sitting in the sun beside her father making dolls with the damp reddish clay he used for making his pots. Geeta never got tired of watching the old man making such beautiful shapes out of clay while his long fingers and the pot he was making went round and round, so smooth and fast. She watched, wide-eyed, until she remembered why she had come.

"Kamala," she whispered, "are you going to the shiny new school?"

"Yes," Kamala answered, "and there I will learn to make pretty clothes for my doll," and she stuck two tamarind seeds into her clay doll to make two black eyes.

Geeta looked at Kamala and couldn't believe her ears. Maybe Kamala's father was *making* her go to school, Geeta thought, and Kamala was pretending not to mind. Geeta was glad she had such a kind father.

She turned her back on Kamala and saw Leela far away drawing water from the well and Geeta ran toward her. Leela was a big girl, twelve years

36

old, and very pretty. Geeta thought she would ask
her about the school.

"Leela, are you going to the shiny new school?"
Geeta asked.

"Of course—and no more water carrying for *me*." Leela tossed her head, almost toppling the pot she balanced on it, and walked away.

Geeta felt very small and sad. Leela didn't seem afraid. Maybe, Geeta thought, it is different if you are a big girl twelve years old and very pretty too, and she went to the place where Balan and his friend Gopal were playing marbles.

"Will you go to the shiny new school, Gopal?"

"Yes, and I am going to be a teacher myself one

day," Gopal answered proudly as he flicked a marble.

Geeta sighed. Maybe it was different if you were a boy.

Under the shade of a big banyan tree Geeta's second best friend, Sarla, and Sarla's mother were weaving yarn into cloth. Geeta watched for a while, helping Sarla to hold the yarn for her mother. Then she asked, "Sarla, you aren't going to the shiny new school, are you?"

"Why not?" Sarla replied gravely. "I will learn so much that I will never be hungry any more."

Geeta did not know what she meant and she could not understand why everyone was willing to go to the school. Her head buzzed and she felt more upset and confused than ever. She wanted to ask all of them about the something called Teacher. If Gopal was going to be one, a Teacher must be a *person*, she thought, and she wanted to ask the others why they were not afraid of him as she was but she felt too shy to ask.

Slowly Geeta walked home, thinking so hard and feeling so confused that she almost bumped into Gopu who was bathing his buffalo. "Gopu, will you also go to——" she began asking him and then stopped because she remembered that Gopu was not afraid of anything, not even of a place that was like a jail (though you could go home at night).

She walked on wondering why no one was afraid—no one but herself. She wondered if she had a wrong memory of what the men had said about the school. But she thought back very carefully and she still remembered the same words. Maybe the men had been wrong.

When she got home her grandfather was dozing on the porch. She would ask him about this school. He would surely know. He was so old and had lived so long that he knew everything. "Grandfather! Grandfather!" She shook him till he woke up. "What is a school?"

"What?" Grandfather blinked and still looked very sleepy.

"What is a Teacher?" Geeta asked him.

Grandfather cupped his hand behind his ear. "What?" he said again. "I can't hear you, child."

Then Geeta knew that Grandfather did not know because whenever he did not understand anything he pretended he did not hear, and she was very sad because there was nobody else to ask.

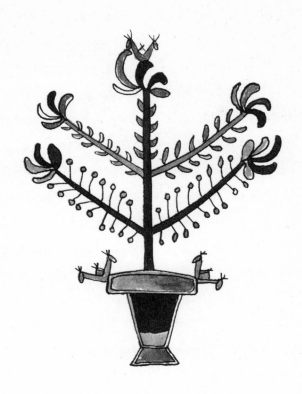

ONE MORNING the next week Geeta's mother woke her up saying, "Today we are going to have a new kind of festival. Come," and she helped Geeta dress very quickly.

Then all of them went to the yard in front of the new school. All the children of the village and the fathers and mothers were there and everyone looked very clean and merry. Gopu's shirt was not torn and

Balan's hands were not dirty and even baby brother's nose was not messy as it often was. Geeta stared at the new building which looked shinier and whiter than ever. How could anything so beautiful be also so terrible, she thought. Then she stopped thinking because a car drove into the village and everyone pressed around to see it. A fat man got out and climbed onto a little platform and spoke to them. He spoke so long that Geeta thought he had one of those funny winding things inside him that would make him go on forever and forever, faster and faster. Everyone called him "Minister-Sir" and seemed very proud of him, but Geeta was glad when he stopped speaking because she did not understand what he said. Then there was music, loud and sweet, and there were flowers and garlands of marigolds and jasmines and roses and, last of all, there was candy for all of them. Geeta loved the music and the flowers and especially the candy but when, at the end of it all, after Minister-Sir had gone, everyone in the village pressed forward to go into the shiny new building and look around their new school, Geeta hung back.

"Come, Geeta," her mother said gently, taking her hand. "Isn't it beautiful? Come, my child."

But Geeta set her chin stubbornly and said, "No." She would not, she thought, go into that place. She never, never would.

She wondered how her friends could go so merrily into a place that was like a jail (though you could go home at night), a place where you had to be clean *all the time* and do exactly as you were told or a person called Teacher would—WHACK!

MANY DAYS passed and still Geeta did not go to the new school. Once her mother said, "Geeta the new school is having a play. Don't you want to go and see it?" Geeta thought she would like to see a play but she was not going into that school and she said, "No."

Every day from her door she saw her friends going to and returning from school, morning and evening, and because they were all laughing and talking it made her feel more lonely and confused than ever. At first she thought they were pretend-ing but they seemed just as cheerful always and you couldn't pretend *every day*. Sometimes they waved to her and shouted, "Aren't you coming to school with us, Geeta?" but she shook her head.

She wanted to ask them about the strange person called Teacher but she was afraid they would laugh at her. Besides, they all seemed very important and busy with their books and pencils and did not seem to have much time to stop and talk or play with her. She thought of how they had all played together so often and she began to feel very lonely indeed. It wasn't much fun playing all by yourself and talking only to yourself.

Then one day, Geeta's mother said Kamala had not gone to school that day because Kamala's mother was sick. So Geeta went to see her. She ran all the way because she had not played with Kamala for so long and it would be good not to be lonely for a while. When she got there, Kamala was sitting in the afternoon sunshine hunched over a book in which she was making strange marks with a pencil.

"Can I play with you today, Kamala?" Geeta asked her.

Kamala looked up absent-mindedly. "What?" she said.

"Will you play with me today, Kamala?" Geeta asked again.

"Oh, no!" Kamala said. "I am too busy. I have

a lot of homework to do," and Kamala returned to her book and her pencil.

Homework! Geeta felt the tears pricking behind her eyelids. Even Kamala, her very best friend, had no time for her. She was alone, all alone, without one friend. She turned and ran down the lane, on and on, past the well and the huts and the water wheel, past the pond and the fields and the mango grove, on and on until—until she did not know where she was and she stopped because she was tired and afraid.

There was a hillock nearby and Geeta climbed to the top of it so that she could see all the better.

But although from the top she thought she could see almost the whole world, still she could not see her village and her home. There was nothing to see but fields and fields and nothing to hear but the sound of the birds' calling. Once she heard a flute but instead of coming nearer it went farther and farther away, and she was alone again and very much afraid.

How she longed to hear the voice of her father as he egged on their lazy buffalo toward the field with slaps on its haunches and shouts of "Hi-yeh!" How she longed to hear her mother calling for her to come home as she did every evening. But there was no sound except the sound of the birds—and—and...!

Suddenly Geeta stood up very straight. There was another sound—very far and faint—but it was slowly getting nearer and louder and it was a new sound. At first it was only a murmur as if her mother were putting her baby brother to sleep; then it was a drone like a very loud bee, and then it was a rumbling like thunder.

She sat very still and listened, wondering where it came from, and then, in the distance, high up in the sky, she saw something glisten, something strange and bright, something she had never seen before. Geeta gazed at it. What could it be? Then she remembered the picture she had seen in the newspaper, the picture of the Silver Bird that was not alive but could fly very fast and carry people through the sky.

Slowly her wonder gave way to a chill of terror. The rumbling was a thundering now. The thing was moving right toward her and she was all alone. She looked up once more, screamed, shut her eyes tight, and ran down the hill faster than she had ever run in her life. She was so frightened that she did not open her eyes and she did not stop running until she bumped into something. Then she had to stop and she opened her eyes, and they grew wider than ever. It was a MAN she had bumped into.

At first Geeta was glad to see someone, especially as this someone looked so nice and kind. But then she began to suppose—SUPPOSE—this man had dropped from the Silver Bird and had come to take her too! She backed away and was about to run again when the man took hold of her arm.

"Why are you running away? What are you afraid of?" the man asked, and he had a voice as kind as his face.

"The Silver Bird," Geeta said and looked up but it had gone.

"What Silver Bird?" The man looked up too.

"That Thing that just flew in the sky. It looked like a monster."

The man smiled. "That was no monster, that was only an airplane!"

"Airplane?" Geeta said. It did not sound so terrible any more.

"Yes. It was built by man to help man, to carry things and letters for him, for you, for all of us, to take us to new towns and countries. Wouldn't you like to see new places?"

Geeta nodded. She thought she would like to see the whole world outside.

"What are you doing all alone here?" the man asked.

"I am lost," Geeta said and she started sobbing, thinking of home and of her mother and father, thinking she might never see all of them again, thinking how it would soon get too dark to see and she would *never, never* find her own village again.

The man patted Geeta on the head. "Don't cry, little one. I will take you home. What is the name of your village?"

Geeta thought very hard and then she said, "I don't know but it has a mango grove and a duck pond and a water wheel that goes c-r-e-a-k, c-r-e-a-k."

The man smiled to himself because there are many hundreds of villages in India and most of them have mango groves and duck ponds and water wheels that creak. So he asked Geeta if there was anything else she remembered about her village.

Then Geeta thought even harder and she said, "Oh, yes! There is a big white shiny new building and it is called a school."

Then the man knew where she lived because,

53

though there are many hundreds of villages in India, there are very few that have big white shiny buildings called schools. He took Geeta's hand in his and they started walking home. And Geeta was no longer afraid.

"Do you like your shiny new school?" the man asked as they walked along.

"I don't go to school," Geeta said.

"Why not?" he asked.

"Just because," she said, the way she had heard Balan say to his friends.

"Why not?" the man asked again. "Don't you want to go to school?"

"No."

The man stopped walking and took both of Geeta's hands in his and said, "Tell me why. You know I am your friend."

Geeta looked into his kind eyes and she said, "I am afraid."

The man looked very serious now, the way her father sometimes looked when Balan had done something wrong. "You were afraid of the Silver Bird because you did not know what it was. That is why you have the new school—to teach you to know more and more and be less and less afraid. You are afraid of school because you do not know what it is. Once you go there you will understand and like it. Will you start going tomorrow with the other children?"

But Geeta set her chin stubbornly and said, "No."

The man said very slowly and very clearly, "Little one, if someone does something for you, won't you do something for him in return, just to say 'thank you'?"

"Yes."

"You were lost and I am going to take you back home. So will you say 'thank you' to me by going to school tomorrow—please?"

Geeta thought of the strange person called Teacher and the place that was like a jail, but she also thought how happy her mother would be if she went to school and she thought how nice it would be to be with Kamala and her other friends again and she thought she wanted to say "thank you" to the kind man. So she looked into the stranger's eyes and she said, "Yes, I will go to the school tomorrow."

And hand in hand they walked back to the village, just as the sun was setting and the fathers were returning from the fields and the mothers were calling for their little ones to come home.

THE NEXT MORNING Geeta woke up long before the cocks and the crows and the buffaloes, and she ran to her mother and said, "Mother, I will go to the shiny new school today."

Happiness shone in her mother's eyes when she heard these words, and she went to a little box where she kept her treasures and from these she took out a dress in cloth of pink silk embroidered with gold thread saying, "I made this dress for you, my daugh-ter, for your first day at school. May it bring you happiness and wisdom."

Then Geeta's mother scrubbed her harder than she had ever done before and when she washed Geeta behind the ears and between her toes—and it tickled and Geeta squealed with delight—her mother said, "See? It's fun to be clean," and Geeta said, "Yes," and she felt very happy to agree with her mother again. Geeta's mother dressed her in the beautiful pink dress and combed her hair extra nicely and put a yellow flower in it and sent her to school with her father and Balan.

All the way to school Geeta's heart went pitapat with excitement. She felt proud of her new dress and proud of walking with her father and when she saw all the other children in the schoolyard, she felt proud to be part of them. But when her father took her into the big, shiny white building and down a long corridor to a room at the end of it, she thought again of the strange person called Teacher and clung to her father with fear in her eyes. Her father opened the door and inside the room there were lots of children and there at the far corner she saw Kamala, her best friend. Her father took Geeta to Kamala and said, "Kamala, look after Geeta as if she were your

own sister," and then, with a pat on Geeta's head, he left.

Geeta felt like running after him but Kamala held her hand saying, "I am so glad you came, Geeta," and then all the other boys and girls came to admire her pretty pink dress and the flower in her hair and she felt a little better.

Kamala showed her all the things in the room— the books with bright pictures in them, the boards

with gaily colored beads, the gray slates and pencils on which you could write anything and wipe it off at once, the lovely pictures on the walls (pictures of many places and animals and birds), a thing like clay which you could turn into any shape, and a huge picture with strange shapes and figures on it which Kamala said was a map—a map of the great world outside. Kamala said the blue was the sea and the brown was the mountains and the green was the plains and fields like their village. Geeta stared at this map and thought it was the most wonderful thing she had ever seen. Then a boy took a chalk and on the blackboard he drew the face of the man with the long drooping mustaches and the man with the head as bald as an egg and the man with the yellow turban and all the boys and girls laughed and Geeta laughed with them. Then someone ran in shouting, "Teacher is coming," and the boy wiped the faces from the blackboard and everyone was very still and quiet.

Geeta felt so frightened again that she held Kamla's hand tight and shut her eyes as she had done when the Silver Bird had flown over her head.

"You must not sleep in class, Geeta," Kamala said, seeing her eyes closed. Slowly Geeta opened her eyes and then she blinked them to make sure she was seeing right. For there at the Teacher's desk stood no fierce stranger but the kind man she had met the day before, the man who had brought her home when she was lost, the man who had taught her not be afraid of the Silver Bird. Geeta thought there was some mistake but Kamala and the other boys and girls were chanting, "Good morning, Teacher," and he was nodding his head. A great gladness swept through Geeta's heart and she sang "Good morning, Teacher," too.

The man put down his books and pencils and said, "Before counting and spelling this morning I would like to talk to you about a wonderful new thing called the airplane which flew close to our village yesterday. Did any of you see it? It looks like a Silver Bird."

Then the teacher looked straight at Geeta and smiled. And Geeta smiled right back because she was so happy that she was no longer afraid of school and of the strange person called Teacher and because she was no longer alone and lonely.